ॐ

American Journal

Other Books by Robert Hayden

American Journal

Poems

by

Robert Hayden

Liveright Publishing Corporation
New York   London

Published simultaneously in Canada
by George J. McLeod Limited, Toronto.
Printed in the United States of America.

First Edition

Library of Congress Cataloging in Publication Data

Hayden, Robert Earl.
   American journal (1913–1980).

   "This edition of American Journal includes ten new
poems."—Liveright Pub. Corp. publicity info.   I.   Title.
PS3515.A9363A74   1980   811'.52   80–36757
ISBN 0–87140–642–X
ISBN 0–87140–127–4 (pbk.)

Liveright Publishing Corporation   500 Fifth Avenue, New York, N.Y.
10110
W. W. Norton & Company Ltd. 25 New Street Square, London EC4A
3NT

1 2 3 4 5 6 7 8 9 0

ဒေါ

For Michael S. Harper,
for William Meredith—
sustainers

Acknowledgments, Notes

I wish to thank Michael S. Harper for permission to include in this new edition of *American Journal* poems first appearing in his Effendi Press edition (1978).

"John Brown" was commissioned by the Detroit Institute of Arts and was first published in *The Legend of John Brown*, a portfolio of reproductions of paintings by Jacob Lawrence, appearing as well in the catalogue for the exhibition of the originals in October 1979. Other poems have been published in the *Michigan Quarterly* and *World Order*.

"The Snow Lamp" is a poem in progress, its subject Peary's expedition to the North Pole in 1909. Its focal character is Matthew A. Henson, co-discoverer of the Pole, who became a legend among the Greenland Eskimos (or Innuit, as they call themselves). They considered him one of their own and named him Miypaluk. The title of the poem comes from an Innuit folktale. The opening section attempts to suggest the spirit and mode of an Eskimo song-poem.

Contents

One

Two

Three

Four

Five

American Journal

One

A Letter from Phillis Wheatley
London, 1773

Dear Obour
    Our crossing was without
event. I could not help, at times,
reflecting on that first—my Destined—
voyage long ago (I yet
have some remembrance of its Horrors)
and marvelling at God's Ways.
    Last evening, her Ladyship presented me
to her illustrious Friends.
I scarce could tell them anything
of Africa, though much of Boston
and my hope of Heaven. I read
my latest Elegies to them.
"O Sable Muse!" the Countess cried,
embracing me, when I had done.
I held back tears, as is my wont,
and there were tears in Dear
Nathaniel's eyes.
    At supper—I dined apart
like captive Royalty—
the Countess and her Guests promised
signatures affirming me
True Poetess, albeit once a slave.
Indeed, they were most kind, and spoke,
moreover, of presenting me
at Court (I thought of Pocahontas)—
an Honor, to be sure, but one,
I should, no doubt, as Patriot decline.
    My health is much improved;
I feel I may, if God so Wills,
entirely recover here.
Idyllic England! Alas, there is
no Eden without its Serpent. Under

the chiming Complaisance I hear him Hiss;
I see his flickering tongue
when foppish would-be Wits
murmur of the Yankee Pedlar
and his Cannibal Mockingbird.
    Sister, forgive th'intrusion of
my Sombreness—Nocturnal Mood
I would not share with any save
your trusted Self. Let me disperse,
in closing, such unseemly Gloom
by mention of an Incident
you may, as I, consider Droll:
Today, a little Chimney Sweep,
his face and hands with soot quite Black,
staring hard at me, politely asked:
"Does you, M'lady, sweep chimneys too?"
I was amused, but dear Nathaniel
(ever Solicitous) was not.
    I pray the Blessings of our Lord
and Saviour Jesus Christ be yours
Abundantly. In his Name,

                    Phillis

John Brown

I
Love feared hated:
aureoled
        in violence.

Foredoomed to fail
in all but the prophetic
task?
        Axe in Jehovah's
loving wrathful hand?

The face is not cruel,
the eyes are not mad but
unsparing;
        the life
has the symmetry
of a cross:
        John Brown
Ossowatomie De Old Man.

II

Doing The Lord's work with sabre
sharpened on the grindstone
of The Word:
Bleeding Kansas:

the cries of my people the cries
of their oppressors harrowed
hacked—poison meat for Satan's
maw.
I slew no man but blessed
the Chosen, who in the name
of justice killed at my command.

Bleeding Kansas:
a son martyred
there: I am tested I am trued
made worthy of my servitude.

Oh the crimes of this guilty
guilty land:
let Kansas bleed.

III
Fury of truth: fury
of righteousness
become
         angelic evil
demonic good?
           My hands
are bloody who never wished
to kill wished only to obey
The Higher Law.
          Fury
of truth, its enigmas,
its blinding
           illuminations.

IV

fire harvest: John Brown
and his Chosen
            at Harper's Ferry:

fury of The Word made pikes guns
swords:
            Arm the slaves
seize their masters kill
only if you must:

bloodburst: bloodflow:

Who sent you here, John Brown?
None in human form.

Fire harvest: harvest fire:

spent forlorn colossal
in that bloody light
death-agonies around him
Gabriel and Nat
awaiting him:
            I have failed:

Come, Death, breathe life
into my Cause, O Death.

V
And now
                these mordant images—

these vibrant stainedglass
colors, elemental shapes
in ardent interplay
with what we know of him
know yet fail to understand—
when we
                for whom he died:

(Shall we not say he died
for us?)

Hanged body turning clockwise
in the air
                the hour
speeding to that hour
his dead-of-night
sorrows visions prophesied:

And now
                these haunting stark
torchlight images:

Theory of Evil

Big Harpe, Little Harpe—
you met them on
the Natchez Trace
you'd stare into mystic
evil's face.
Oh wouldn't live
to say you had,
or if you lived
could only gasp
with hurting breath—
Them Harpes—
before delirium and death

Po' wayfaring
stranger, none
to ease his moans,
Big Harpe slashed
him open, filled
his belly with stones
then left him for
the river to eat.

(We think of that
as we follow the Trace
from Nashville down
to Jackson—muse
on the cussedness
of the human race.)

When Big Harpe's head
had been cut off,
they took and nailed it
to a sycamore tree.
(Buzzards gathered
but would not feed.)
It crooned in its festering,
sighed in its withering—
Almighty God
He fashioned me
for to be a scourge,
the scourge of all humanity.

Two

Paul Laurence Dunbar
for Herbert Martin

We lay red roses on his grave,
speak sorrowfully of him
as if he were but newly dead

And so it seems to us
this raw spring day, though years
before we two were born he was
a young poet dead.

Poet of our youth—
his "cri du coeur" our own,
his verses "in a broken tongue"

beguiling as an elder
brother's antic lore.
Their sad blackface lilt and croon
survive him like

The happy look (subliminal
of victim, dying man)
a summer's tintypes hold.

The roses flutter in the wind;
we weight their stems
with stones, then drive away.

Homage to Paul Robeson

Call him deluded, say that he
was dupe and by half-truths betrayed.
I speak him fair in death,
remembering the power of his
compassionate art. All else fades.

The Rag Man

for Herbert

In scarecrow patches and tatters, face
to the wind, the Rag Man walks
the winter streets, ignoring the cold
that for weeks has been so rigorous
we begin to think it a punishment
for our sins—a dire warning at the very least.

He strides on in his rags and word-
less disdain as though wrapped in fur,
noted stranger who long since
(the story goes) rejected all
that we risk chills and fever and cold
hearts to keep. Who is he really, the Rag Man?

Where is he going or coming from?
He would not answer if we asked,
refusing our presence as he would
our brief concern. We'd like to buy
him a Goodwill overcoat, a bowl of soup;
and, yes, we'd like to get shut of the sight of him.

The Prisoners

Steel doors—guillotine gates—
of the doorless house closed massively.
We were locked in with loss.

Guards frisked us, marked our wrists,
then let us into the drab Rec Hall—
splotched green walls, high windows barred—

where the dispossessed awaited us.
Hands intimate with knife and pistol,
hands that had cruelly grasped and throttled

clasped ours in welcome. I sensed the plea
of men denied: Believe us human
like yourselves, who but for Grace. . . .

We shared reprieving Hidden Words
revealed by the Godlike imprisoned
One, whose crime was truth.

And I read poems I hoped were true.
It's like you been there, brother, been there,
the scarred young lifer said.

The Tattooed Man

I gaze at you,
longing longing,
as from a gilt
and scarlet cage;
silent, speak
your name, cry—
Love me.
To touch you, once
to hold you close—
My jungle arms,
their prized chimeras,
appall. You fear
the birds-of-paradise
perched on my thighs.
Oh to break through,
to free myself—
lifer in The Hole—
from servitude
I willed. Or was
it evil circumstance
that drove me to seek
in strangeness strange
abiding-place?
Born alien,
homeless everywhere,
did I, then, choose
bizarrity,
having no other choice?

Hundreds have paid
to gawk at me—
grotesque outsider whose
unnaturalness

assures them they
are natural, they indeed
belong.
But you but you,
for whom I would
endure caustic acids,
keenest knives—
you look at me with pain,
avert your face,
love's own,
ineffable and pure
and not for gargoyle
kisses such as mine.
Da Vinci's Last Supper—
a masterpiece
in jewel colors
on my breast
(I clenched my teeth in pain;
all art is pain
suffered and outlived);
gryphons, naked Adam
embracing naked Eve,
a gaiety of imps
in cinnabar;
the Black Widow
peering from the web
she spun, belly to groin—
These that were my pride
repel the union of
your flesh with mine.
I yearn I yearn.
And if I dared
the agonies

of metamorphosis,
would I not find
you altered then?
I do not want
you other than you are.
And I—I cannot
(will not?) change.
It is too late
for any change
but death.
I am I.

Three

Elegies for Paradise Valley

I

My shared bedroom's window
opened on alley stench.
A junkie died in maggots there.
I saw his body shoved into a van.
I saw the hatred for our kind
glistening like tears
in the policemen's eyes.

iI
No place for Pestalozzi's
fiorelli. No time of starched
and ironed innocence. Godfearing
elders, even Godless grifters, tried
as best they could to shelter
us. Rats fighting in their walls.

III
Waxwork Uncle Henry
(murdered Uncle Crip)
lay among floral pieces
in the front room where
the Christmas tree had stood.

Mister Hong of the
Chinese Lantern (there
Auntie as waitress queened it
nights) brought freesias, wept
beside the coffin.

Beautiful, our neighbors
murmured; he would be proud.
Is it mahogany?
Mahogany—I'd heard
the victrola voice of

dead Bert Williams
talk-sing that word as macabre
music played, chilling
me. Uncle Crip
had laughed and laughed.

IV

Whom now do you guide, Madam Artelia?
Who nowadays can summon you to speak
from the spirit place your ghostly home
of the oh-riental wonders there—
of the fate, luck, surprises, gifts

awaiting us out here? Oh, Madam,
part Seminole and confidante
("Born with a veil over my face")
of all our dead, how clearly you
materialize before the eye

of memory—your AfroIndian features,
Gypsy dress, your silver crucifix
and manycolored beads. I see
again your waitingroom, with its wax
bouquets, its plaster Jesus of the Sacred Heart.

I watch blue smoke of incense curl
from a Buddha's lap as I wait with Ma
and Auntie among your nervous clients.
You greet us, smiling, lay your hand
in blessing on my head, then lead

the others into a candlelit room
I may not enter. She went into a trance,
Auntie said afterward, and spirits
talked, changing her voice to suit
their own. And Crip came.

Happy yes I am happy here,
he told us; dying's not death. Do not grieve.
Remembering, Auntie began to cry
and poured herself a glass of gin.
Didn't sound a bit like Crip, Ma snapped.

V

And Belle the classy dresser, where is she,
who changed her frocks three times a day?
    Where's Nora, with her laugh, her comic flair,
    stagestruck Nora waiting for her chance?
Where's fast Iola, who so loved to dance
she left her sickbed one last time to whirl
in silver at The Palace till she fell?
    Where's mad Miss Alice, who ate from garbage cans?
    Where's snuffdipping Lucy, who played us 'chunes'
on her guitar? Where's Hattie? Where's Melissabelle?
    Let vanished rooms, let dead streets tell.

Where's Jim, Watusi prince and Good Old Boy,
who with a joke went off to fight in France?
    Where's Tump the defeated artist, for meals or booze
    daubing with quarrelsome reds, disconsolate blues?
Where's Les the huntsman? Tough Kid Chocolate, where
is he? Where's dapper Jess? Where's Stomp the shell-
shocked, clowning for us in parodies of war?
    Where's taunted Christopher, sad queen of night?
    And Ray, who cursing crossed the color line?
Where's gentle Brother Davis? Where's dopefiend Mel?
    Let vanished rooms, let dead streets tell.

VI

Of death. Of loving too:
Oh sweet sweet jellyroll:
so the sinful hymned it while
the churchfolk loured.

I scrounged for crumbs:
I yearned to touch the choirlady's hair,
I wanted Uncle Crip

to kiss me, but he danced
with me instead;
we Balled-the-Jack
to Jellyroll

Morton's brimstone
piano on the phonograph,
laughing, shaking the gasolier
a later stillness dimmed.

VII
Our parents warned us: Gypsies
kidnap you. And we must never play
with Gypsy children: Gypsies
all got lice in their hair.

Their queen was dark as Cleopatra
in the Negro History Book. Their king's
sinister arrogance flashed fire
like the diamonds on his dirty hands.

Quite suddenly he was dead,
his tribe clamoring in grief.
They take on bad as Colored Folks,
Uncle Crip allowed. Die like us too.

Zingaros: Tzigeune: Gitanos: Gypsies:
pornographers of gaudy otherness:
aliens among the alien: thieves,
carriers of sickness: like us like us.

VIII

Of death, of loving,
of sin and hellfire too.
Unsaved, old Christians
gossiped; pitched

from the gamblingtable—
Lord have mercy on
his wicked soul—
face foremost into hell.

We'd dance there, Uncle
Crip and I,
for though I spoke
my pieces well in Sunday School,

I knew myself (precocious
in the ways of guilt
and secret pain)
the devil's own rag babydoll.

Four

Names

Once they were sticks and stones
I feared would break my bones:
Four Eyes. And worse.
Old Four Eyes fled
to safety in the danger zones
Tom Swift and Kubla Khan traversed.

When my fourth decade came,
I learned my name was not my name.
I felt deserted, mocked.
Why had the old ones lied?
No matter. They were dead.

And the name on the books was dead,
like the life my mother fled,
like the life I might have known.
You don't exist—at least
not legally, the lawyer said.
As ghost, double, alter ego then?

Double Feature

At Dunbar, Castle or Arcade
we rode with the exotic sheik
through deserts of erotic flowers;
held in the siren's madonna arms
were safe from the bill-collector's power.

Forgave the rats and roaches we
could not defeat, beguiled by jazzbo
strutting of a mouse. And when
the Swell Guy, roused to noblest wrath,
shot down all those weakéd men,

Oh how we cheered to see the good we were
destroy the bad we'd never be.
What mattered then the false, the true
at Dunbar, Castle or Arcade,
where we were other for an hour or two?

The Dogwood Trees
(for Robert Slagle)

Seeing dogwood trees in bloom,
I am reminded, Robin,
of our journey through the mountains
in an evil time.

Among rocks and rock-filled streams
white bracts of dogwood
clustered. Beyond, nearby, shrill slums
were burning.

the crooked crosses flared. We drove
with bitter knowledge
of the odds against comradeship we dared
and were at one.

Letter

It was as though you struggled against
fierce current jagged with debris
to save me then. I am desperate still.
Old age—the elegy time—that brings
a sense of shores receding? But no.
What rends my spirit like beast-
angel, angel-beast has for
a lifetime nurtured and tormented me.

—This tells you nothing, tells you all,
leaves unresolved a thing absurd,
in truth grotesque. You have risked pain
because of it, are yet compassionate.
I will no longer ask for more
than you have freely given or can give.

Ice Storm

Unable to sleep, or pray, I stand
by the window looking out
at moonstruck trees a December storm
has bowed with ice.

Maple and mountain ash bend
under its glassy weight,
their cracked branches falling upon
the frozen snow.

The trees themselves, as in winters past,
will survive their burdening,
broken thrive. And am I less to You,
my God, than they?

"As my blood was drawn"

As my blood was drawn,
as my bones were scanned,
the People of Bahá
were savaged were slain;

skeletons were gleaning
famine fields,
horrors multiplying
like cancer cells.

World I have loved,
so lovingly hated,
is it your evil
that has invaded
my body's world?

As surgeons put
me to the knife,
innocents
were sacrificed.

I woke from a death
as exiles drowned.
I called on the veiled
irradiant One.

As spreading oilslicks
burned the seas,
the doctors confirmed
metastasis.

World I have loved
and loving hated,
is it your sickness
luxuriating
in my body's world?

In dreams of death
I call upon
the irradiant veiled
terrible One.

Killing the Calves

Threatened by abundance, the ranchers
with tightfaced calculation
throw the bawling calves into a ditch and
shoot them in order to fatten the belly of cost.

The terror of the squandered calves mingles
with the terrible agony of the starving
whom their dying will not save.
Of course, the killing is "quick and clean";
and though there is no comparison reminds us

nonetheless—men women children
forced like superfluous animals
into a pit and less than cattle
in warcrazed eyes like crazed cattle slaughtered.

The Year of the Child
(for my Grandson)

And you have come,
Michael Ahman, to share
     your life with us.
We have given you
     an archangel's name—
and a great poet's;
     we honor too
Abysinnian Ahman,
     hero of peace.

     May these names
be talismans;
     may they invoke divine
magic to protect
     you, as we cannot,
in a world that is
     no place for a child—

     that had no shelter
for the children in Guyana
     slain by hands
they trusted; no succor
     for the Biafran
child with swollen belly
     and empty begging-bowl;
no refuge for the child
     of the Warsaw ghetto.

What we yearned
but were powerless to do
        for them, oh we
will dare, Michael, for you,
        knowing our need
of unearned increments
        of grace.

    I look into your
brilliant eyes, whose gaze
        renews, transforms
each common thing, and hope
        that inner vision
will intensify
        their seeing. I am
content meanwhile to have
        you glance at me
sometimes, as though, if you
        could talk, you'd let
us in on a subtle joke.

    May Huck and Jim
attend you. May you walk
        with beauty before you,
beauty behind you, all
        around you, and
The Most Great Beauty keep
        you His concern.

The Point
Stonington, Connecticut

    Land's end. And sound and river come
together, flowing to the sea.
    Wild swans, the first I've ever seen,
cross the Point in translucent flight.
    On lowtide rocks terns gather;
sunbathers gather on the lambent shore.

    All for a moment seems inscribed
on brightness, as on sunlit
    bronze and stone, here at land's end,
praise for dead patriots of Stonington;
    we are for an instant held in shining
like memories in the mind of God.

Zinnias
for Mildred Harter

Gala, holding on
    to their harvest and wine
        colors
with what seems
    bravura
        persistence:

    We would
    scarcely present
bouquets of them
    to Nureyev
        or Leontyne Price:

Yet isn't
    their hardy elan one way
        of exclaiming
More More More
    as a gala
        performance ends?

The Islands
for Steve and Nancy, Allen and Magda

Always this waking dream of palmtrees,
magic flowers—of sensual joys
like treasures brought up from the sea.

Always this longing, this nostalgia
for tropic islands we
have never known and yet recall.

We look for ease upon these islands named
to honor holiness; in their chromatic
torpor catch our breath.

Scorn greets us with promises of rum,
hostility welcomes us to bargain sales.
We make friends with Flamboyant trees.

Jamaican Cynthie, called alien by dese lazy
islanders—wo'k hahd, treated bad,
oh, mahn, I tellin you. She's full

of raucous anger. Nevertheless brings gifts of
scarlet hibiscus when she comes to clean,
white fragrant spider-lilies too sometimes.

The roofless walls, the tidy ruins
of a sugar mill. More than cane
was crushed. But I am tired today

of history, its patina'd cliches
of endless evil. Flame trees.
The intricate sheen of waters flowing into sun.

I wake and see
the morning like a god
in peacock-flower mantle dancing

on opalescent waves—
and can believe my furies have
abandoned for a time their long pursuit.

Five

from THE SNOW LAMP

it is beginning oh
it begins now
breathes into me
becomes my breath

out of the dark
like seal to harpoon
at breathinghole
out of the dark

where I have wait-
ed in stillness that
prays for truth-
ful dancing words

ay-ee it breathes
into me becomes
my breath spiritsong
of Miypaluk

he who returned to us
bringing festive speech
Miypaluk hunter of seal
and walrus and bear

and who more skilled
at building sledge
and igloo   ay-ee
the handler of dogs

the pleaser of girls
Miypaluk who came
from the strange-
ness beyond the ice

he who was Inouk
not knowing one of us
Inouk returned
to his people　ay-ee

Miypaluk Miypaluk

II

Across lunar wastes of wind and snow
Yeti's tract
                 chimera's land
horizonless
                 as outer space

through ice-rock sea
and valley
                 (palm tree
fossils locked
in paleocrystic ice)

through darkness dire
as though God slept
in clutch of nightmare

through crystal and copper light
welcome as the smoking blood
of caribou
                 desolate
as the soul's appalling night
toward Furthest North
                             where all
meridians end
                 toward

(cairn)

No sun these months. Ice-dark and cold.
Blind howling. Demonic dark that storms
the soul with visions none visionless can bear.
We are down to the last of the pemmican. Soon
must kill and eat our dogs.

The Angakok chants magic words against
evil spirits. Prepares for his descent
into the sea, there to comb the maggots from
Queen Nerrivik's hair that she send up her fish
(her chopped-off fingers) and seals lest we starve.

We struggle against the wish to die.
We use the Eskimo women to satiety, by this act
alone knowing ourselves men, not ghosts. We have
cabin fever. We quarrel with one another over
the women, grow vicious (as the childish Eskimos
do not). We are verminous. We stink like Eskimos.
We fight our wish to die.

Astronauts

Armored in oxygen,
        faceless in visors—
mirrormasks reflecting
        the mineral glare and
shadow of moonscape—
        they walk slowmotion
floatingly the lifeless
        dust of Taurus
Littrow. And Wow, they
        exclaim; oh boy, this is it.

They sing, exulting
(though trained to be wary
        of "emotion and
philosophy"), breaking
        the calcined stillness
of once Absolute Otherwhere.

Risking edges, earthlings
        to whom only
their machines are friendly
        (and God's radar-
watching eye?), they
        labor at gathering
proof of hypothesis;
        in snowshine of sunlight
dangerous as radium
        probe detritus for clues.

What is it we wish them
to find for us, as
        we watch them on our
screens? They loom there
        heroic antiheroes,
smaller than myth and
        poignantly human.
Why are we troubled?
        What do we ask of these men?
What do we ask of ourselves?

[American Journal]

here among them   the americans   this baffling
multi people   extremes and variegations   their
noise   restlessness   their almost frightening
energy   how best describe these aliens in my
reports to The Counselors

disguise myself in order to study them unobserved
adapting their varied pigmentations   white black
red brown yellow   the imprecise and strangering
distinctions by which they live   by which they
justify their cruelties to one another

charming savages   enlightened primitives   brash
new comers lately sprung up in our galaxy   how
describe them   do they indeed know what or who
they are   do not seem to   yet no other beings
in the universe make more extravagant claims
for their importance and identity

like us they have created a veritable populace
of machines that serve and soothe and pamper
and entertain   we have seen their flags and
foot prints on the moon   also the intricate
rubbish left behind   a wastefully ingenious
people   many it appears worship the Unknowable
Essence   the same for them as for us   but are
more faithful to their machine made gods
technologists their shamans

oceans deserts mountains grain fields canyons
forests   variousness of landscapes weathers
sun light moon light as at home   much here is
beautiful   dream like vistas reminding me of

home   item   have seen the rock place known
as garden of the gods and sacred to the first
indigenes   red monoliths of home   despite
the tensions i breath in i am attracted to
the vigorous americans   disturbing sensuous
appeal of so many   never to be admitted

something they call the american dream   sure
we still believe in it i guess   an earth man
in the tavern said   irregardless of the some
times night mare facts we always try to double
talk our way around   and its okay the dreams
okay and means whats good could be a damn sight
better   means every body in the good old u s a
should have the chance to get ahead or at least
should have three squares a day   as for myself
i do okay   not crying hunger with a loaf of
bread tucked under my arm you understand   i
fear one does not clearly follow i replied
notice you got a funny accent pal   like where
you from he asked   far from here i mumbled
he stared hard   i left

must be more careful   item   learn to use okay
their pass word   okay

crowds gathering in the streets today for some
reason obscure to me   noise and violent motion
repulsive physical contact   sentinels   pigs
i heard them called   with flailing clubs   rage
and bleeding and frenzy and screaming   machines
wailing   unbearable decibels   i fled lest

vibrations of the brutal scene do further harm
to my metabolism already over taxed

The Counselors would never permit such barbarous
confusion   they know what is best for our sereni
ty   we are an ancient race and have outgrown
illusions cherished here   item   their vaunted
liberty   no body pushes me around i have heard
them say   land of the free they sing   what do
they fear mistrust betray more than the freedom
they boast of in their ignorant pride   have seen
the squalid ghettoes in their violent cities
paradox on paradox   how have the americans
managed to survive

parades fireworks displays video spectacles
much grandiloquence much buying and selling
they are celebrating their history   earth men
in antique uniforms play at the carnage whereby
the americans achieved identity   we too recall
that struggle as enterprise of suffering and
faith uniquely theirs   blonde miss teen age
america waving from a red white and blue flower
float as the goddess of liberty   a divided
people seeking reassurance from a past few under
stand and many scorn   why should we sanction
old hypocrisies   thus dissenters   The Counse
lors would silence them
a decadent people The Counselors believe   i
do not find them decadent   a refutation not
permitted me   but for all their knowledge

power and inventiveness not yet more than raw
crude neophytes like earthlings everywhere

though i have easily passed for an american   in
bankers grey afro and dashiki long hair and jeans
hard hat yarmulka mini skirt   describe in some
detail for the amusement of The Counselors   and
though my skill in mimicry is impeccable   as
indeed The Counselors are aware   some thing
eludes me   some constant amid the variables
defies analysis and imitation   will i be judged
incompetent

america   as much a problem in metaphysics as
it is a nation earthly entity an iota in our
galaxy   an organism that changes even as i
examine it   fact and fantasy never twice the
same   so many variables

exert greater caution   twice have aroused
suspicion   returned to the ship until rumors
of humanoids from outer space   so their scoff
ing media voices termed us   had been laughed
away   my crew and i laughed too of course

confess i am curiously drawn   unmentionable   to
the americans   doubt i could exist among them for
long however   psychic demands far too severe
much violence   much that repels   i am attracted
none the less   their variousness their ingenuity
their elan vital   and that some thing   essence
quiddity   i cannot penetrate or name